Dear Parent:

Congratulations! Your child is taking the first steps on an exciting journey. The destination? Independent reading!

STEP INTO READING® will help your child get there. The program offers five steps to reading success. Each step includes fun stories and colorful art. There are also Step into Reading Sticker Books, Step into Reading Math Readers, Step into Reading Phonics Readers, Step into Reading Write-In Readers, and Step into Reading Phonics Boxed Sets—a complete literacy program with something for every child.

Learning to Read, Step by Step!

Ready to Read **Preschool–Kindergarten**
• big type and easy words • rhyme and rhythm • picture clues
For children who know the alphabet and are eager to begin reading.

Reading with Help **Preschool–Grade 1**
• basic vocabulary • short sentences • simple stories
For children who recognize familiar words and sound out new words with help.

Reading on Your Own **Grades 1–3**
• engaging characters • easy-to-follow plots • popular topics
For children who are ready to read on their own.

Reading Paragraphs **Grades 2–3**
• challenging vocabulary • short paragraphs • exciting stories
For newly independent readers who read simple sentences with confidence.

Ready for Chapters **Grades 2–4**
• chapters • longer paragraphs • full-color art
For children who want to take the plunge into chapter books but still like colorful pictures.

STEP INTO READING® is designed to give every child a successful reading experience. The grade levels are only guides. Children can progress through the steps at their own speed, developing confidence in their reading, no matter what their grade.

Remember, a lifetime love of reading starts with a single step!

© 2013 Viacom International Inc. and Viacom Overseas Holdings C.V. All rights reserved.
Published in the United States by Random House Children's Books, a division of Random House,
Inc., 1745 Broadway, New York, NY 10019, and in Canada by Random House of Canada Limited,
Toronto. Step into Reading, Random House, and the Random House colophon are registered
trademarks of Random House, Inc. Nickelodeon, Teenage Mutant Ninja Turtles, and all related
titles, logos, and characters are trademarks of Viacom International Inc. and Viacom Overseas
Holdings C.V. Based on characters by Peter Laird and Kevin Eastman.

Visit us on the Web!
StepIntoReading.com
randomhouse.com/kids

Educators and librarians, for a variety of teaching tools, visit us at RHTeachersLibrarians.com

ISBN 978-0-449-81826-8 (trade) – ISBN 978-0-375-97175-4 (lib. bdg.)

Printed in the United States of America   10 9 8 7 6 5 4 3 2 1

STEP INTO READING®

STEP 4

TEENAGE MUTANT NINJA TURTLES

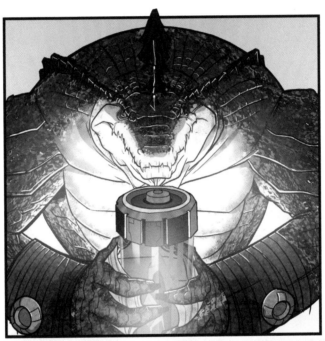

MIKEY'S MONSTER

Adapted by Hollis James

Illustrated by Patrick Spaziante

Based on the teleplay "Leatherhead" by Ron Corcillo and Russ Carney

Random House 🏠 New York

A giant creature was loose in the Kraang's secret hideout.

The Kraang were blobby brain-like invaders from another dimension. They lived in robot exoskeletons and spoke strangely.

A team of Kraang-droids chased after the creature, firing their laser blasters.

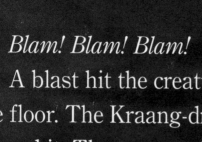

Blam! Blam! Blam!

A blast hit the creature. It fell to the floor. The Kraang-droids gathered around it. The monster looked like a giant alligator. It clutched a glowing object in one claw.

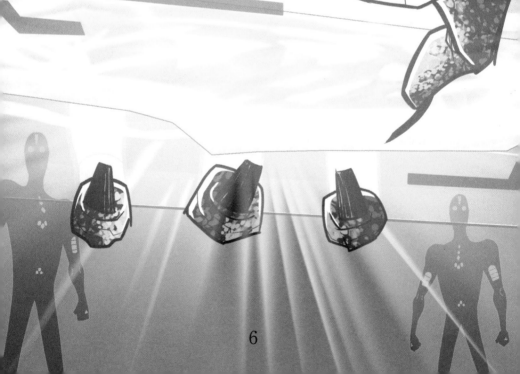

"Give to Kraang the power cell that Kraang demands that you give to Kraang!" said the head Kraang-droid.

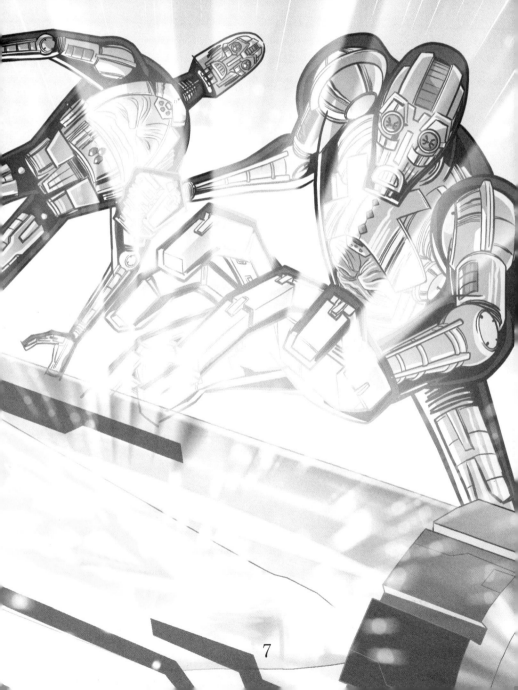

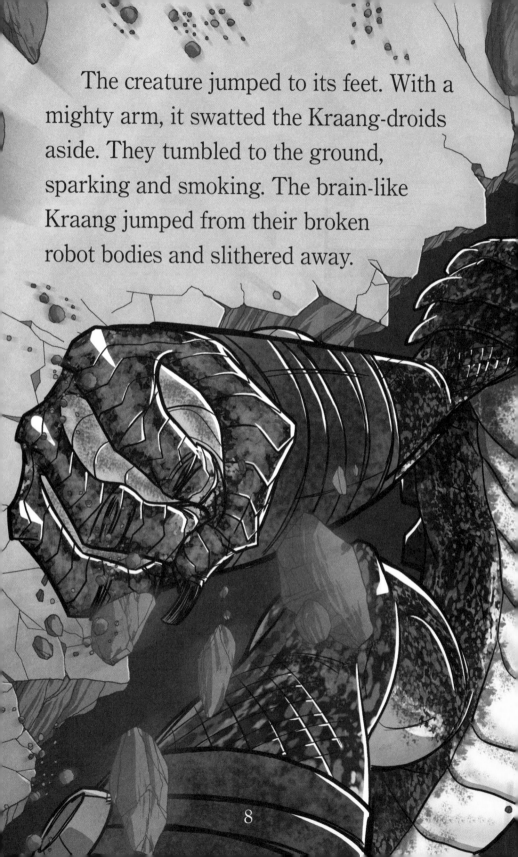

The creature jumped to its feet. With a mighty arm, it swatted the Kraang-droids aside. They tumbled to the ground, sparking and smoking. The brain-like Kraang jumped from their broken robot bodies and slithered away.

The creature punched a hole
in a wall and escaped.

Six months later, Leonardo, Raphael, and Donatello were watching the news in their secret underground lair. Michelangelo bounded into the room.

10

"Who wants to try my latest creation from the kitchen?" he asked. "We all love pizza. We all love milk shakes. So I combined them! I call it a *P-shake*!"

The other Turtles groaned.

On TV, a reporter began a story about the sewers. The Turtles turned to watch.

"I'm Joan Grody with a sewer shocker!" the reporter said. "Were city workers attacked . . . by a giant monster?"

The reporter said the sewers would
be searched. That was bad news for the
Turtles and their secret lair.

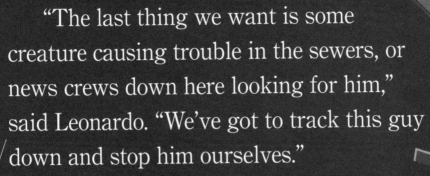

"The last thing we want is some creature causing trouble in the sewers, or news crews down here looking for him," said Leonardo. "We've got to track this guy down and stop him ourselves."

"There's a tunnel number in the news report," said Donatello. "It's tunnel 281."

"Let's go!" said Leonardo.

The Turtles quickly found the tunnel. The only sign of the strange creature was a few large footprints.

"What the heck made these footprints?" asked Leonardo.

"Feet," said Michelangelo. "Really big feet."

Suddenly, the Turtles heard brutal
battle sounds echoing through the sewers.
They charged down the tunnel
to investigate.

The Turtles turned a corner and saw a giant mutant alligator battling a group of Kraang-droids. The alligator grabbed two Kraang-droids and smashed them together. With a powerful swipe of its tail, it sent another Kraang-droid flying into a wall. A pink Kraang brain-thing scurried out of the broken robot.

"Awesome!" Raphael said.

"Wow, I never thought I'd feel sorry for the Kraang," whispered Donatello.

One Kraang-droid fired a massive blaster cannon at the raging creature. The blast hit the creature in the chest and dropped him to the ground.

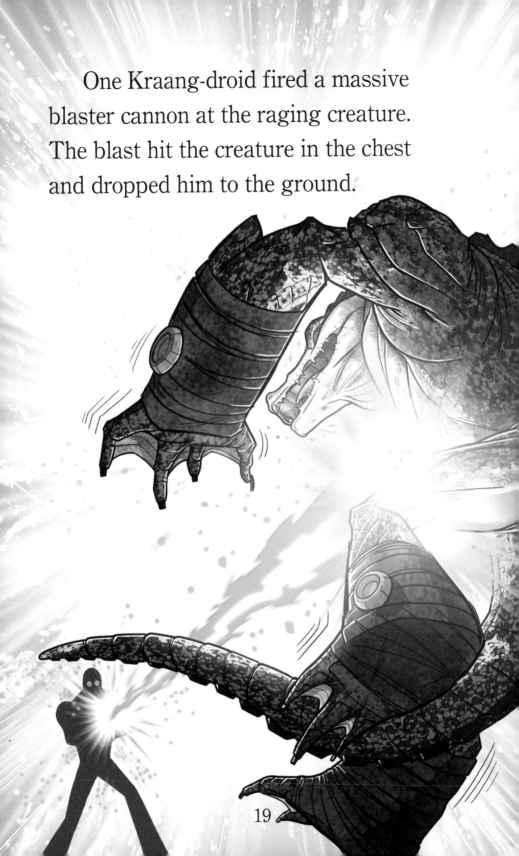

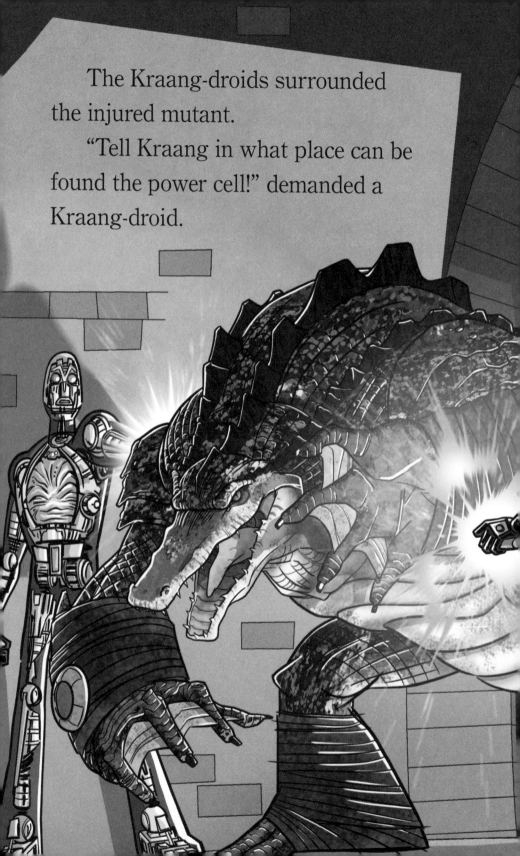

The Kraang-droids surrounded
the injured mutant.

"Tell Kraang in what place can be
found the power cell!" demanded a
Kraang-droid.

"Never!" screamed the creature.

"Then Kraang will continue to inflict pain," said another Kraang-droid.

"We've got to help him," Michelangelo whispered. He was about to jump into action, but Leonardo grabbed him.

Mikey, we don't know anything about that guy," said Leonardo. "He could be more dangerous than the Kraang."

But Michelangelo couldn't stand by while the creature was being hurt. He sprang into battle.

Crack!

He knocked one Kraang-droid out with a blow from his *nunchucks*. A flying kick toppled another.

Leonardo, Raphael, and Donatello couldn't let their brother fight alone.

"Let's go whack some piñatas," Raphael grunted as the rest of the Turtles charged into the fight.

Donatello swung his *bo* staff.
Leonardo's swords flashed like lightning.
The Kraang-droids were quickly
overwhelmed and ran away.

"What do we do with him?"
Michelangelo asked. "We can't leave
him here."

The other Turtles didn't want to
bring the creature home with them,
but Michelangelo talked them into it.

Back at the lair, Donatello wanted to chain the creature, but Michelangelo said that would be wrong. The Turtles began to argue.

"What's all the commotion?" asked Splinter as he entered the room.

"Mikey brought home a dangerous monster just because it was hurt!" said Raphael.

"There is no monster more dangerous than a lack of compassion," responded Splinter.

The Turtles told Splinter about the creature's fight and the power cell the Kraang wanted.

"You made a wise decision, Michelangelo," said Splinter. The Turtles were shocked to hear this. "I can't believe I just said that, either," he continued. He told Michelangelo to chain the creature for the time being. "We need to learn what he knows about the Kraang."

Splinter sent Leonardo, Donatello, and Raphael to look for the missing power cell. They returned to tunnel 281. All they found was garbage.

"If I were an alligator," Donatello said, "I'd hide something underwater."

The three Turtles dove into the grimy sewer water.

Meanwhile, back in the lair, the giant alligator woke up. He strained against his chains.

"Set me free!" he roared.

Michelangelo calmly introduced himself. "My brothers and I saved you from the Kraang. We brought you home with us so you could get better."

Michelangelo fed the creature his homemade pizza-noodle soup.

"This is the best thing I have ever tasted!" said the creature.

"All right!" said Michelangelo. "Somebody finally likes my cooking!"

The creature and Michelangelo became friends. Michelangelo undid the chains and gave the creature a name: Leatherhead.

31

Deep in the sewers, Leonardo, Raphael, and Donatello came out of the water and entered a room filled with dangerous booby traps. They had to act quickly to avoid getting hurt. They ducked under flying street signs and jumped over rolling manhole covers.

The Turtles made it safely into the next room and found the power cell behind a secret door.

"Any idea what the Kraang would use this for?" asked Leonardo.

Donatello inspected it. "It could power anything—a flashlight, a blaster cannon, even a city on the moon!"

Leonardo, Raphael, and Donatello brought the power cell back to the lair. They couldn't believe Michelangelo had unchained the giant alligator.

"What if he goes berserk?" Leonardo asked.

"Don't worry," Michelangelo replied. "Leatherhead is totally mellow."

But when Leonardo mentioned the Kraang, Leatherhead exploded with rage. "KRAANG!" he roared.

When Leatherhead saw the power cell, he grew even angrier.

"Thief!" he growled. He started to fight the Turtles for the power cell.

"Stop!" Splinter commanded. "Get away from my sons!"

Leatherhead lunged for Splinter, but Splinter was too fast for him. The giant mutant stopped fighting, snatched the power cell, and ran away.

Michelangelo chased Leatherhead
until they reached an old subway car in an
abandoned station. It was Leatherhead's
home.

"Dude!" Michelangelo said sternly.
"Friends don't beat up friends!"

"I'm sorry," said Leatherhead. "There
are forces in me I can't always control."

Leonardo, Raphael, and Donatello found Michelangelo just as Leatherhead was starting his story.

"The Kraang found me as a young gator," he said. "They took me to their dimension, mutated me, and tried to turn me into a living weapon."

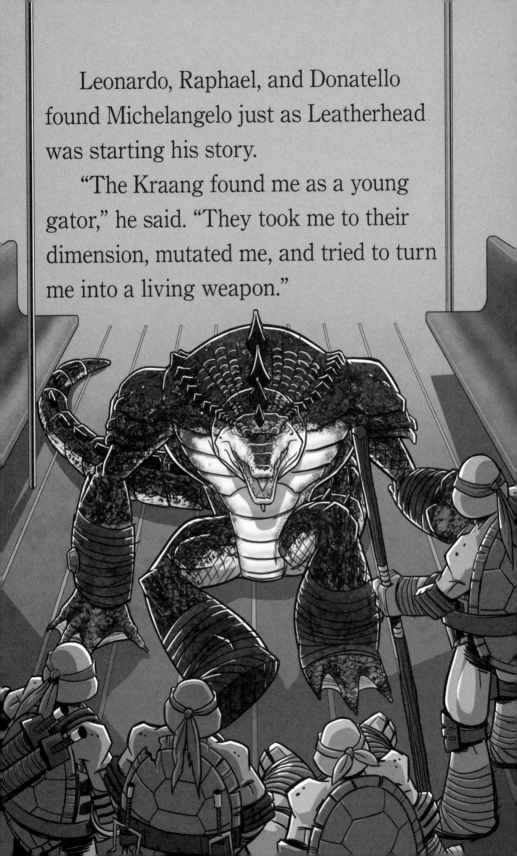

Leatherhead explained that he had stolen the cell that powered the Kraang's portal to Earth and escaped. He wanted to stop other Kraang from entering this dimension.

Suddenly, a blast rocked the train car. It was the Kraang-droids!

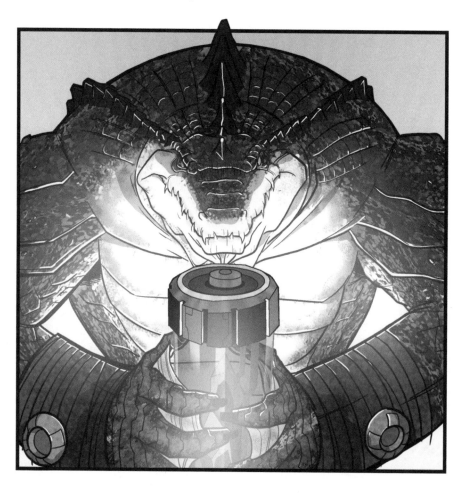

"Give to Kraang the power cell!"
a robot voice ordered.

"Donnie, can you get this subway car
running?" asked Leonardo.

Donatello said he couldn't because
there was no electricity.

Leatherhead handed the power cell to Donatello.

"You have trusted me," said Leatherhead. "Now I am trusting you."

With that, he hopped out the train door to fight the Kraang.

Michelangelo, Leonardo, and Raphael
fought off the Kraang that smashed
through the windows. Donatello tried to
connect the power cell to the train's engine.
"I think I got it!" he exclaimed.
The last wire sparked as it touched
the cell.

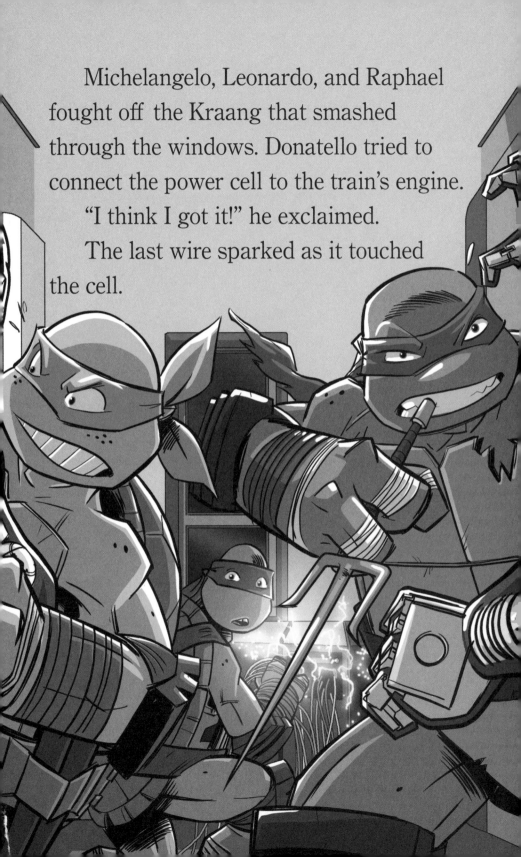

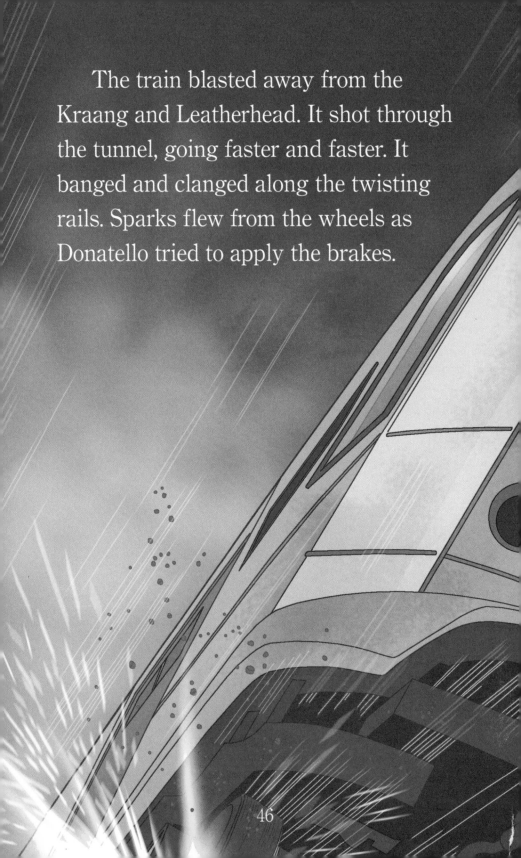

The train blasted away from the
Kraang and Leatherhead. It shot through
the tunnel, going faster and faster. It
banged and clanged along the twisting
rails. Sparks flew from the wheels as
Donatello tried to apply the brakes.

The car finally screeched to a stop. The Turtles were safe for now, but they were worried. They hoped Leatherhead was okay. They knew the Kraang would come looking for their power cell.

The battle with the Kraang would continue another day.